Steven Black and the Tales from Beyond

Steven Black and the Tales from Beyond

The Orb of Possibility

J.O.Welch

FernByd Books

To Josh
Who heard the stories first.

Part I.

I sit in a dark cave, seeing nothing except the faint glow of a torch about fifteen feet away. The cave is damp and quiet. I hear nothing but the small dripping noise of water falling off a stalactite behind me. Looking around with fear in my heart, I am tied down to a small wooden chair, and a sudden smell of decay fills my nose.

Abruptly, an arm breaks out of the ground, and the only reason I can see it is because the arm is darker than the rest of the shadows in the room. The hand of the arm makes a motion like that of someone controlling a hand puppet. A sound comes out from the hand as it moves its top four fingers up and down on its thumb. It speaks in a strange unrecognizable dialect, yet somehow, I understand what it's saying to me.

It declares, *The War of the Watchers will come along, but with its end evil will rise at dawn. A friend of the old will betray your trust, and with this betrayal, all will rust. Beware these words that you hear now, for if you don't, to the evil power all men will bow.*

After it finishes reciting the creepy verse, another arm bursts out from the ground. It set its hand down on the floor and begins pushing up. Then, a head emerges from the rock. It has two eyes and a jack-o-lantern smile that glows a bright yellow.

The creature begins crawling toward me, repeating my name, *Steven.* I try to escape the chair but to no avail. *Steven.* I try kicking at the beast, but my leg passes right through it. *Steven*! it yells before it lunges toward me.

Then I awake. Sitting up with a start, I am lying on my bed in my little room. Níta Conifer, my friend who is the manifestation of the spirit of a young tree, otherwise known as a nymph, is sitting on my bed poking my face and yelling "Steven!" while I was sleeping as an attempt to wake me.

"What! What do you want?" I ask rubbing my eyes.

"I'm hungry," Níta responds.

I sigh and roll out of bed.

My room is a huge mess. My bed isn't made. My desk on the other side of the room is cluttered and has my laptop still open. The bookshelf next to my bed has books pouring out of it, and the floor has seemed to turn into a keeping place for all my miscellaneous items.

I walk toward the back of my room, toward a desk full of strange, enchanted, and technological items. Walking to the right of the desk, I pull a lever on the wall. The floor under the desk opens, and the desk slides into the gap while a kitchen sink and stove take its place.

"Ok, what do you want to eat?" I ask Níta.

"Pancakes!" she responds.

"Níta, you don't even eat the pancakes! Or any food for that matter. You just kind of stare at it," I remark.

"I eat the spirit of the food," she shoots back like it's an obvious fact.

"Food items don't have spirits," I reply.

"Well, you didn't think that about trees until you first found me! So how would you know?" She responds, with a hint of sass.

Nymphs are just the manifestation of the spirit of a plant, I think to myself. Meaning, that Níta herself is the "ghost" of a potted sapling presenting herself as a young human girl. While this seemingly does make a case for her only eating the "spirit" of food, it doesn't explain how non-plant based items like pancakes can have a spirit.

I shake my head and make pancakes for Níta. I then go to pour myself some cereal but discover I'm out of milk.

Quietly, I lay my head on the table with a groan and mumble to myself, "Today's going to be a bad day."

I dress in a t-shirt, jeans, and a jacket, and head out to the west meeting room. The hallway from my room is like a hotel hallway, a long wide stretch of space with doors lining the walls. After a quick walk to the elevators, I push one of the buttons and began to head down to the bottom floor of the Watcher headquarters.

While descending, the elevator stops, and the doors open. In steps Mia Pippin, one of my best friends. She's a species known as the Hūcca, the only one of her kind in the Watcher headquarters. She looks humanoid, but her skin is blue, and she has antlers protruding out of her long brown hair. She's dressed in a cute pink tank top and some sweat pants like she was about to go on a morning run.

She's been my friend ever since she first arrived here about a year and a half ago. For when she first arrived at the Watcher headquarters, it had been discovered that she was a natural portal maker, a type of Watcher who creates portals using either magical energy or a specific gene in their body. Not to mention, she's great in the field of technology, and an excellent fighter.

Unfortunately, when she came to the Watcher HQ, her portals had stopped working, so she couldn't become a Watcher. The Watcher Governors decided to put her on public portal duty, a giant technological portal that can be used to bring a large group to a single destination for a fee. Mia was then assigned to train with me in both fighting and in helping her regain her portal making abilities. After that, we quickly became friends.

While she is very shy, she is also very sweet. She has taught me a lot about fighting and technology, which is an area that I was not very familiar with.

As the elevator doors close, she timidly waves, "Hi Steven."

"Hey," I respond

In the elevator, I ask her, "So how did the promotion testing go?"

She takes a long sigh and says, "Not good. Even though I did well on my fighting and academic portions of the test, I can't be promoted to official Watcher unless I figure out how to use my portals again!"

Not being able to create portals has taken its toll on Mia. I feel partially responsible. I was assigned to help her regain portal ability, but I can't seem to be able to figure it out.

"I'm sorry about that," I reply.

"You know, I've been thinking about just disguising myself and trying to go live in the village of men down the mountain since this Watcher thing isn't exactly working out," Mia says.

"No, you can't do that!" I argue. "Don't give up yet, it's only been a year. If we keep trying I know that we'll learn how to get your portals back!"

Mia smiles a little. "Thanks, Steven."

"No problem," I add.

"Any luck regaining your memories?" Mia asks me.

I shake my head. When I first came to the Watcher's HQ, I unexpectedly lost all my memories. For years, I've been searching the multiverse looking for a way to cure my amnesia, but no luck so far.

"Well," Mia continues, "If you believe that I'll get my portals back, then you should believe that you'll get your memories back!"

I smile, "Thanks, Mia."

She smiles back.

The doors of the elevator open.

"I'll see you later," I tell Mia.

She waves her hand in goodbye as the elevator doors close.

Exiting the elevator, I walk through the ginormous library that fills up most of the Watcher HQ. The library is a three-story room filled with rows and rows of bookshelves. You see, Watchers travel universes and record what we witness. So, after over two million earth years of recording everything a plethora of people witnessed, the amount of information begins to stack up.

Within the library, I see multiple Watchers reading books, and studying up on the next world they're about to visit. A Rookie Watcher who had just read a book with what appears to be a dinosaur symbol on the front is now breathing heavily into a paper bag in the corner, surrounded by friends trying to calm him down. Just another day in the life of a Watcher, I think to myself.

At the end of the west side of the library, I walk through two doors into the meeting room already filled with people talking amongst themselves. I see my oldest friend in the room, Rick Davis. Rick is the first Watcher I met when I first came to the HQ over ten years ago. He's a Science Portal Maker, a type of Watcher that creates portals using technology, and he's one of the few human Watchers I personally know. He's tall with dark chocolate-colored skin and curly black hair. Rick has an almost impish grin, but he's one of the nicest guys, I know, and my best friend. I go and sit next to him.

"Hey," I say to him.

"Hey man!" he answers.

We sit and start to chat.

"Did you hear about that explosion that happened down in one of the higher north-west dorms?" he asked me.

"Oh yeah!" I exclaim. "I live three floors below where that happened!"

"How *did* that happen anyway?" he asks.

"I believe it might have been a portal malfunction, at least that's what I heard," I guess.

Before Rick can respond, the doors to the room fly open and Komo Yong walks in. Komo Yong is a Science Portal Maker, like Rick, but a huge jerk. He's humanoid but he has lizard scales, claws, jagged teeth, yellow eyes with slits for pupils, and a lizard tail. He wears a ridiculous lab coat and goggles that he never uses. Instead, they remain resting on his head. He comes and sits across from me and Rick.

"Hey, Komo," Rick waves.

Komo looks at him, "Sup." He begins to glare at me. "Why are you hanging out with a 'Natural,' Rick?" he asks him still glaring at me.

I furrow my brow, "Rick and I have been friends for a good ten years Komo, and he doesn't care whether or not his friends create portals using technology or magic."

Komo looks back at Rick, "Sure, but our project calls for Science Portal Makers only. We shouldn't surround ourselves with bad influences."

I get angry. "What's your problem man? Do you have any respect for anyone except yourself?"

Komo shrugs. He gets up and moves to the other end of the table. Good riddance.

"It sucks that you had to get paired up with him for your project thingy," I tell Rick after Komo leaves.

"Actually, I choose him to be part of my group." He corrects me.

I stare at Rick, "Why on Ixlamca would you ever voluntarily choose Komo to be your partner?"

"Because he has a lot of great ideas! Sure, he's a

little rude to Natural portal makers, but he has had some problems with them in the past."

I stare at Komo from across the room, "Well that may just be his own fault."

Rick shrugs and turns toward the front of the room where the headmaster of the North-West quadrant of Watchers just walked in. Our Head Master's name is Ethan Kratos, but we just call him "Mr. K-". He's a huge burly man with a thick white beard who always wears a suit and a fedora. Think Kingpin mixed with Santa Claus and Odin, that's probably what Mr. K looks like.

He goes through his normal monthly speech

"The MVW (Most Valuable Watcher) is... blah... blah... Watcher portal fluid production is down by... blah... blah... keep up the excellent work, except for you Billy... blah... blah... blah..." and so forth.

Once he's done, he dismisses the meeting.

But then he says, "Steven, please come see me in my office."

A little worried, I head toward his office directly behind the meeting room.

Once in his office, he looks up at me from his desk.

"Come in, sit down," he says to me.

"Did I do something wrong?" I ask.

"That depends," he says.

"On what-"

I'm cut off by Mr. K lifting what looks like a ray gun and pointing it at my chest. Instinctively, I throw my hands up.

Mr. K asks me in a calm but stern voice "Steven, did you cause the explosion on the 34th floor in room F:453 of the North-west Watcher HQ quadrant?"

"What, I-" I stammer.

"Answer me." Mr. K says sternly.

"No, I didn't!" I exclaim.

Mr. K then puts his finger on the trigger and pulls it. I shut my eyes, but nothing happens. I open my eyes to see Mr. K using the ray gun to shine a long green light on me, scanning my features. Once done, the scanner emits an electronic voice stating, "Truth" and the machine turns off. Mr. K sits back in his chair.

"Steven," he says, "I have a mission for you."

Still slightly shocked, I respond "W-what?"

Mr. K grins "I apologize for the lie detector, but I just had to be sure. You see, Steven, there is evidence pointing toward the idea that the explosion might have been set up by a Watcher terrorist to cause fear and panic in the Watcher headquarters."

My head feels like it's spinning. "Ok, that's a lot of information. I thought the explosion was just an accident caused by a faulty electronic portal maker?"

"That's what I thought as well." Mr. K responds. "But I uncovered this from the scene!"

He then lifts a plastic bag holding a tiny bottle full of green liquid. "This is Extracted Possibility. The main component found in ultra-destructive bombs!"

I examine the bottle, "Couldn't someone use that stuff for an alternative use?"

"Oh, sure!" Mr. K continues, "This stuff is used in portal fluid, so that's where my mind first went to, but the thing is, the explosion came from the room of a Professional *Natural* Portal Watcher known as Jim Welsh. If he had lost his portal making ability, he would've just came to the Watcher governors, and they would've treated him. And upon further questioning of his friends and family, it was revealed that he was never experimenting with Extracted Possibility. So, someone must have placed this in his room and set off a makeshift bomb to kill him, sadly they succeeded."

"So," I inquire, "what do you need me for?"

Mr. K smiles. "I need you to find out who did this!"

"Me!?" I exclaim, a bit confused. "Why me? I'm just an Amateur Watcher!"

"Exactly!" Mr. K roars with delight. "You are the most trustworthy one in my quadrant who has the right amount of skill! I don't trust any of the Professional Watchers. They'd be able to fake a lie detector test, and any Rookie Watcher wouldn't have the necessary talent for the mission. It must be investigated. Whoever is doing this may continue the attacks and may even cause an epidemic! If you accept, here are the universal codes that you will need." He then hands me a small piece of paper with some universal codes written on them.

All the pieces started to click in my head, but I still had one question. "Aren't there other amateur

Watchers you could send? I still feel like I may not be the best choice."

Mr. K smirked, reached into his desk drawer, and said, "Well, there may be something in it for you. I know that you have lost a decent amount of your memories from before your time here as a Watcher, so here."

He gives me a letter that reads,

"Dear Ethan Kratos,

We understand that you are trying to find the one who attacked your headquarters. While we can confirm that your quadrant was attacked, even we are blind to whom it was who attacked you. So, any hero that you deem worthy of finding this terrorist will be gifted with *The Orb of Possibilities*. This orb will give them anything that they wish (granted that the wish doesn't commit mass genocide or rearrange the flow of time). We all hope that you find whoever attacked your quadrant and we will be watching over the hero whom you choose.

Sincerely,
Chronos: Celestial of Time."

My hand begins to shake, and my heart races. Mr. K says exactly what I am thinking,

"If you succeed, you will remember everything."

A huge smile begins to grow on my face.

"So, are you in?" Mr. K asks me.

"Yes!" I exclaim.

"Good." Mr. K says as his face grows serious and he leans in very close. "Tell no one about this." He says as his mouth slips back into a smile. "And may El Qubekī guide you."

I nod and walk out of the office happier than I have ever been in my whole life.

Part II.

As I run through the library preparing to research the universes I'll need to visit, I run into

Mia. Literally! We collide, both of us falling flat on the floor. She drops a bag and I nearly poke my eye out with one of her antlers.

"Oh, Mia! Sorry." I say.

"It's ok." She responds. "Why are you running up and down the library?"

I blush, "Sorry, something cool just happened and I'm a bit excited."

"I can tell," she laughs.

I notice the bag on the floor next to her. "What's that?"

She grabs the bag, "Oh, it's just my lunch."

"Lunch? It's only 10 a.m. though."

Mia looks at her watch, "Actually, it's 2 p.m. You've been in here running around for about 4 hours."

"Oh. I may have gotten a little carried away." I say.

Mia nods. "You want to come and eat lunch with me?"

"Sure."

We head toward the cafeteria. We find a seat, then we begin to chat.

"So, what's this big opportunity you're excited about?" She asks.

"Sorry, but I'm not really supposed to talk about it, It's classified," I respond.

"Oh." Mia frowns, "Ok, I understand."

For a minute I look around the room, and then I look back at Mia.

"Translator off?" I ask her,

"Translator off." She agrees.

We both take a small device out from behind our ears and set it down on the table. All the Watchers at the HQ wear this Multiversal translator that allows us to communicate with each other and with beings from separate worlds. But, before we had these translators, some long-forgotten Watcher invented a language known as "Lukīxcj" or "Watchish" in English. Us Watchers don't need it anymore, but Mia and I learned it, so we could discuss things in secret without anyone eavesdropping.

"*Ok,*" I begin in Watchish, "*after the meeting with Mr. K, he called me into his office. He told me that he has a special mission for me. Remember that explosion that happened a few days ago?*"

"*Yeah, wasn't that just an accident?*" Mia responds.

"*That's what I thought as well! But according to Mr. K, the explosion was caused by a Watcher on the inside!*" I whisper.

"*No! There's no way!*" Mia exclaims in disbelief.

"*There is a way, and according to Mr. K, if I manage to find who attacked the HQ, I'll be gifted the Orb of Possibilities,*" I say.

Mia's jaw drops. "*Wait, with the Orb of Possibilities, you'll be able to-*"

We continue in unison, "*Regain my lost memories!*"

"*Yep!*" I exclaim.

We place our translators back on. "Just make sure not to tell anyone ok?" I ask.

Mia nods. "Do you already have some books for the worlds you need to travel too?"

"Yep," I respond as I hand her some of the books I collected.

Even though Mia isn't a Watcher yet, she knows her universes like the back of her sky-blue hand. Mainly because she spends a lot of her free time in the library.

She glances over the first book. "Oh, well it seems like you're going to start pretty close to home."

"Yeah, the first mission called for Ixlamca," I reply.

Ixlamca is the name of the Watchers residing universe, labeled as universe $D^2*3:9045$. While we aren't technically from here, it's the main meeting point for any universe traveling being. It's your typical run of the mill high fantasy world.

As Mia continues to scan the books, she asks me "What are you trying to find exactly?"

"The eternal flame." I answer, "I'm having a little trouble finding where it is though."

"Here it is," Mia says immediately, pointing to a spot on the map. "58 munsins East of Mount Walkaī. It's in that Orc guarded cave in the forest clearing."

"Whoa," I say, impressed by Mia's knowledge, "How'd you find that so fast?"

"Read about it the week I arrived here." She replies with a grin.

I smile. "Thanks for the advice," I tell her.

"Glad I could be of help." She smirks.

We keep chatting until we finish our lunch, then I head back to my dorm room.

Once in my room, I open my door and begin to pack for my trip. I grab some water, food, an invisibility potion that is hanging on the rack on the wall, two mini transmogrifying machines, a few silver pieces, and my sword.

My sword is one of my most prized possessions. It is named Thorn. It has a gold handle and a long two-sided blade with magic Norse runes written on it. The runes give it the ability to destroy its target with a single hit if the wielder wishes it, but it may only be done once every two moons. I sheath it on my belt.

I look over toward my bed and see Níta lying asleep face first in a wide-open book. I write a note telling her I'll be away, and place it on the cover of her book.

I pick up the note Mr. K gave me. It says I need to bottle a piece of the eternal flame. I go and stand in front of my rug, focus all my energy on one spot, and picture the outside of Ixlamca in my mind. I see the matter in front of me begin to swirl and distort. Then, with a ripping sound, a portal appears on my rug. The portal is a round oval, I can see the soft earth of a forest clearing on the other side, but the picture is distorted, like a forever rippling pool of water. I jump in.

Once on the other side, I take in my surroundings. I stand on top of a hill surrounded by trees. Vast forestry encases me, and the world seems to be completely green.

Using the tracking device on my arm, I make my way through the forest until the device leads me to a dark cave in the side of a cliff.

There is a collection of Orcs guarding the cave, so much so that it would be impossible to try and take them all out myself.

I need to find another way into the cave, I think to myself, But where would I go?

Suddenly, I notice a gleaming coming from my right, a bright blue gleaming emitting from the clasped hands of a small goblin wearing a torn tunic and a pair of trousers. His cracked glasses stand perched upon the tip of his nose.

I realize that the creature must have been able to get into the cave through a separate entrance, or else he would have been caught.

Silently, I creep behind the goblin and whisper, "Hey buddy."

The creature suddenly jumps and scurries away. Before he could get too far, I create a portal underneath him and another on the tree next to me. The goblin comes flinging out of the portal and crashes into a bush across the way.

I run over to him and I begin to hear him grumbling in a high pitched gravelly voice, "Nasty Watcher, making Keener fly through the air. Put out blue fire."

"You know what Watchers are?" I ask the goblin named Keener. My shock stems from the rarity of any beings in Ixlamca having any clue what Watchers are at all.

Keener ignores my question, "What does Watcher want? Watchers only talk to Keener anymore if need something."

I am frankly perplexed by the little goblin and his amount of knowledge on the Watchers. But I decide to get back to the point of my quest. "Are you able to get me into the cave without alerting any of the Orcs? I saw you with the eternal flame in your hands."

The goblin thinks for a moment, "If Keener shows you entrance, will Watcher leave Keener alone?"

I nod my head.

Keener gestures his head "Follow."

He leads me around the back of the cave and into a smaller entrance obscured by vines and bushes. Inside, the smell of the dark damp cave hits my nostrils.

"Ok, you can go," I tell Keener. He begins to scurry back out the exit, but before he leaves, he looks back at me with his big grey eyes, a curious glint passes through them as he stares at me. Suddenly, he shakes his head and scurries away.

Ignoring my confusion I continue my way down the cave.

I make it to the end of the cave rather quickly. Once at the end, I see a pedestal with a flame on the top, shining a bright blue. The flame is huge and stretches nearly to the ceiling, yet as I got nearer, the cave grew cooler. At the foot of the pedestal, I take out a jar from my bag and place it upside down into the roaring flame. Immediately, the flame fills the jar as I quickly screw the lid into place. The pedestal remains lit with a huge flame.

I begin to create a portal to leave, but something behind me makes a noise, like that of breathing. I turn to look at it, and I see the Hand from my dream last night. I take a step back out of fear. Am I asleep? Is this all a dream? I go to pinch myself, but I don't wake up. This is real. The hand begins to move its "mouth."

It tells me, *Steven, save me!*

The ground below it begins to widen, and it creates a hole. Within the hole, I see a sea of monsters of unimaginable horror. Floating right below the hole is the rest of the shadow man with the jack-o-lantern smile staring up at me. The hand speaks again, but as it does the yellow mouth and eyes of the shadow man glow in unison with the words.

Save me, Steven! You could prevent this! This is real Steven! It will be real! Don't tell me, Steven! Don't tell me!

It may have kept on talking, but I'm already making a portal back to my room. I jump in, leaving the shadow man behind.

As I exit the portal, my heart races at an extreme rate. I turn around and close the portal. I can't risk letting it in. That thing is real. It was in Ixlamca! This wasn't a dream. This time it was real!

I turn toward my bed and see Níta still sleeping on top of her book, the note I wrote had fallen onto her face. She lay there blissfully unaware of my adventures and what I had just encountered. A small smile forms on my face. I go over to her, place the blanket over her, take the note off her face, and slide the book from under her. I tab her place and look at the cover of the book. It's titled "How to be a Healer for dumb-dumbs." I place it back on my shelf and head out of my room.

I ride the elevator up to the library. Once I exit, I walk through the library corridors. The moon gently shines through the windows. The halls are empty except for the occasional nocturnal Watcher. I scour the shelves for the next books I need. Once I find them, I clutch them under my arm and decide to head out to the balcony.

Once there, I look over the railing and see the mountains across the horizon. They seem to stretch on infinitely. The moon shines brightly above the mountains illuminating the two villages amidst the forestry below. The two villages symbolize the unity of the men and lesser elves. They are connected by a road stretching over the country border for safe travel and trade. The Watcher headquarters was placed directly on the mountain acting as a middle point for the border between the countries.

I find myself lost to the beauty of it all until something catches my attention out of the corner of my eye. A man stands in the shadows of the balcony. At first, fear seeps into my heart for I believe it is the shadow man, but as he steps into the light, he reveals himself to only be Rick.

"Hey man." He begins to say, but he notices the fear in my eyes. "You ok?" He asks. "It's just me you know. I ain't gonna hurt you."

I begin to calm down. "Sorry, I just... had a stressful day."

He comes and stands next to me. "I see." He responds. "If I didn't know any better, I would guess that you just witnessed something traumatizing." He says with that slight impish grin.

"How did you know? My constant shaking or my rapid heartbeat?" I ask sarcastically.

"Neither." He responds. "Shaky breath." He continues.

I chuckle a little and continue to stare out at the villages. "What do you think they're doing down there," I ask.

Rick shrugs. "Honestly, I've got no clue. You know, for such a primitive group of people, you'd think they'd worship us as their gods;"

I look at Rick. "They aren't primitive! I've met them myself. They've got huge advanced cities as well. And besides, I think our founder, Dr. Spencer, went down to them and told them to not think of us as gods, just as 'a different kind of mortal.'"

"Why would he do that? Give up the opportunity for a form of godhood?" Rick asks.

"Well, he was a strong believer in El Qubekī," I respond, "It would be a bit strange claiming to be a god when you believe in an all-powerful creator deity."

"Well you don't believe that stuff, right?" Rick asks.

"I do actually."

"Really? Why?"

I look at Rick, "Our daily lives consist of traveling near infinite universes finding all sorts of wonderful, magical, and fantastical things, and you think that all of that doesn't have some sort of creator behind it?"

"Well, I have an alternative theory." Rick shoots back, "I think when the multiverse started, these balls of energy came together and became sentient! They split up the multiverse and became known as the gods! You know like Zeus, and Thor, and all them. We even have gods here in Ixlamca!"

"Yes, but those gods have beginnings! Sure, they're immortal, but they still began one way or another. They are tied to the universe they belong to. El Qubekī is not. Who's to say he didn't create these god-like beings to just live in his worlds and create similar to what us mortals do? And maybe they started calling themselves 'gods' after mortals began worshiping them, making them arrogant?"

Rick stares at me, "Where did you hear all of this?"

"Dr. Spencer wrote a book about it. Found it in the library."

Rick looks at me and shrugs again. "I don't know. Maybe I just like the idea of being a god that's appreciated." He says.

I laugh. "Of course, you would. If you were a god, you'd be the god of appreciation. 'blessing people with the appreciation they deserve.'"

As I say this, I move my hand like I'm using a wand on somebody. Rick laughs and pushes me a bit. In doing so he accidentally knocks the books out of my hand. When I go to pick them up again, he looks at the books and then back at me.

"Ullr, huh?" he asks me.

"Yep," I tell him.

"Isn't that where your little tree friend is from?" Rick asks.

I nod in response.

"Might want to keep that journey a secret." He tells me.

I nod. Níta has been wanting to go to Ullr forever. It is a human-less world filled only with nymphs and mythological creatures. She hasn't been since she was just a seed, but I don't want her to go yet. You never know what might happen in Ullr.

"Why are you going there?" Rick asks me.

I wonder for a moment whether I should tell him. "*Tell no one about this.*" That's what Mr. K said. I had already broken that rule by telling Mia, but I'd trust her with my life. The thing about Rick is that he isn't the best at keeping secrets. If I tell him and he spreads the info to the wrong person, the consequences could be catastrophic.

"It's classified," I tell him.

"Oh?" he asks.

"Ordered by the big K himself." I continue.

Ricks' eyes widen. He looks almost confused, but then his face changes to a state of realization. He turns and looks down off the balcony. In the light of the moon, he looks almost evil. But he puts his smile back on and turns back to me.

"Good luck with that!" he tells me.

"Thanks," I respond.

We chat for a little while longer, then I head back inside.

Once back in my room, I place my books on the

desk. Níta's leaves had returned to her tree, so she was no longer on my bed. I go and lay down on it.

Before I can fall asleep, I remember the shadow monster. What if it returns in my sleep? Could it hurt me? I ponder these things for hours. But despite my worry, I fall asleep.

Lucky for me, the shadow man decided to evade my dreams during the night. But, when I woke up, Níta was once again standing over me, this time she has an angry look on her face with her arms crossed.

"What?" I ask.

"Ullr!" she yells holding one of my books I got last night above me. "You're going to Ullr without me again!"

Oh great, I think.

"Look Níta, I'm going there on a special mission, it's very dangerous," I tell her.

"Dangerous, shmane-gerous," she reply's "How can thousands of other nymphs live there and survive, but it's too 'dangerous' for me!"

I sigh, "Look we've discussed this, I'll take you when you're older. Now's just not a good time."

Níta sighs, and then goes and sits at the desk, and begins to mumble to herself.

I get up, make breakfast for both of us, and get dressed.

"You know," Níta begins to say, "If you brought me along I could show you how good I've gotten at healing,"

I smirk. "Ok, if I come back with a cut I'll see if you can heal it," I say sarcastically.

Níta frowns. "You're mean"

I smile while I begin to create a portal. "Thanks," I reply.

Then I jump into the world of Ullr.

Once on the other side, I quickly close the portal behind me to keep Níta from coming through. The world of Ullr stands before me. I've been here a few times before, but I can never get over how beautiful it is. The entire landscape is covered with snow, and trees surround me.

I realize the fact that these trees have nymphs in them, and that they are probably watching me right now. I shake off the eerie feeling. I have a mission to do.

I take out the note that was given to me by Mr.

K and read it. "Find the kettle hidden by the goat. " Weird verse, but Mr. K was never one for poetry.

Obviously, I need to find a Faun. But the question is which Faun. There are thousands of them in Ullr, not to mention that I am fairly sure most of them own kettles. But before I could move, I hear footsteps behind me. I turn around to see a Faun carrying nothing but an umbrella.

I am startled by his sudden appearance that I jump back a bit, but I must've scared the Faun a bit more as he screams and tumbles into the snow.

The faun and I stare at each other for a moment. Suddenly I say, "Did you hide a kettle?"

The faun stares at me for a minute.

"Pardon?" he responds.

"I'm looking for a Faun that hid a kettle."

The Faun's eyes lit up.

"Oh! I knew this day would come! You are the one I was told about! A human from worlds beyond would come and ask for my enchanted kettle! Oh yes!"

I looked him over for a bit.

"Who told you that?" I asked him.

He responds, "Why the great god Eru told me

of course! He told me to hide it and to 'lead the human from beyond to it,' oh yes he did!"

I smiled. "Well, I guess you're the Faun I was looking for," I say.

The Faun frowns. "Oh, I don't mean to be rude, but I'm no Faun, I'm a Satyr. Sure, we're terribly similar, but still different at that."

"Oh, sorry," I tell him.

"Oh, that's alright." The Satyr replies. "What's your name?" he asks.

"I'm Steven," I respond.

"Steven." He repeats. "What a peculiar name!"

I smile again at the delightful Satyr.

"And what is your name?" I ask.

The Satyr replies, "My name is Prem Shifim! But you could just call me Prem."

"Cool name," I say. "Now, could you lead me to the kettle?" I ask him.

"Oh yes! Right this way!" replies Prem.

He leads me through the forest as the snow falls on us. He offers me to come under his umbrella, but I decline. After about a half-hour of walking, we come across a small cave.

"The kettle is in there!" Prem says gleefully.

I walk into the cave. We keep going in deeper and deeper until it's so dark I can't see a thing. My foot hits something metallic, and I feel around at my feet for what I had hit. It was defiantly the kettle from what I could feel, and it pulsed with some sort of magical aura. I stuff it in my bag.

I hear Prem sigh, and whisper, "I'm sorry, Steven."

"For what?" I asked a bit confused.

"For this." He replies.

I then feel a sharp pain in the back of my head, as if someone had just hit me with a baseball bat at full force. I crumble to the ground.

"Don't worry." I hear Prem say to himself. "It'll help Ullr in the end. You're ok with this."

And with that, I am hit in the back of the head again. Then everything fades to black.

Part III.

I see myself halfway up Mount Walkaï, Home of the Watchers. I am scraped up from head to toe. I look weary and tired from traveling. I remember that day. Ten years ago, I crawled my way up the mountain. Only sixteen years old. I wasn't very familiar with my portals yet, so I couldn't just teleport up there. I climbed my way past rocks and jagged shards. It took three days to make it completely up the mountain.

This must be a dream, I think. This is my earliest memory, but I'm watching it from a third-person point of view.

I watch myself as I begin to reach the top. Looking up, I see the giant Watchers HQ in front of me. The place is huge. I can only see the door and the wall beside and above it. Even though the top is invisible from here, I know it's built like a castle.

I stand up. I limp toward the door. Frantically, I knock. The person who answers the door is Rick.

"Can I help you?" he asks.

I collapse on the floor from exhaustion. When I wake up, I'm lying in bed. There are some bandages on my body, a beeping noise emits from a machine next to me, and no one else is in the room.

After a while, I am let out of the healing area. Once I step into the library, my jaw drops. Never had I seen such a vast room with new books and people at every turn. I am so lost in the sight that I don't even realize someone is standing right next to me.

"Oh hey, you're up!" Rick tells me.

I jump at his voice. "Yeah, I guess I am."

"I'm Rick." He tells me, with his familiar impish grin, "What's your name?"

"I-I'm Steven," I say.

"So, Steven, where you from?"

I am about to answer, but then I hesitate, "I-I don't know."

"Oh." Rick looks at me a bit worried, "Well, either way, you're not from this universe, are you?"

"No, I don't think I am," I reply.

"Well, then I guess I'll have to show you around

the place." He begins walking off gesturing for me to follow.

He shows me around the library while I gape at everything I see. At one point, while walking through an aisle, Rick notices a book with strange text on it that I could not read. He grabs the book.

"You can read that?" I ask

"Oh, don't worry, we'll get you an inter-universal translator soon enough, but lucky for you, I speak English, so you don't need one when talking to me." He smirks.

While reliving this through my dreams, I still am unable to read the text on the book, but now something about it seems familiar.

Rick continues to guide me through the HQ. After that, he leads me to my room.

"Thanks for showing me around," I tell him.

Rick smiles, "Hey no problem. I'll see you around."

I realized from then on, Rick and I would become best friends. He walks away, and I close the door, as my dream fades away.

I awake to the sound of dripping. I look up and see a smoldering torch about 15 feet away from me.

Everything else around me is dark. I try to move, but I'm tied down to a chair. Oh no. It's the cave from my dream.

I try to untie the ropes tying me down, but I feel what seems like the dull end of a blade touching my wrist. Without hesitation, I scoot the chair up, lean onto my legs, spin the chair around, and kick the thing that was behind me. The creature falls back, and I catch a glimpse of the outline of a knife in its hands.

But then, I hear a familiar voice say "Ow! What the Heck?!"

I stare at the outline of the person for a second, then I notice the vague shape of a tail behind it.

"Komo?" I ask.

The creature takes out a match and lights it, revealing himself to be in fact, Komo Yong.

"Dude!" I exclaim. "Why did you kidnap me!?"

"I didn't kidnap you!" Komo yells in his annoying voice. "Well, at least not personally, but it wasn't my idea! So, I'm trying to save you now!" He gestures toward his knife.

I stare at him. "What?"

Komo sighs. "Look, this is a matter of life and

death! Not just for you or me, but for every single Watcher!"

I stare at him. "Then why are you here? And why am I tied up to a chair?"

Komo looks around nervously. "There's no time to explain! I must cut you out of here! He tied the knots too tight, so I can't just untie them."

I look confused. "Who are you working for?" I ask.

"*Were* working for." Komo corrects me.

I roll my eyes. "It doesn't matter. Just tell me the problem."

Komo anxiously looks around again. "Ok, the person I'm working for is bent on creating strife between the Science and the Natural Portal Watcher factions. He created a group, they call themselves 'The Revelation.' They're the ones who murdered Jim Welsh, and when they discovered that you are trying to stop us, they sent that Satyr to lead you to us."

I angrily stare at Komo. "You joined a Watcher terrorist group and tried to murder me?!" I yell at him.

Komo puts his hands up in defense "I didn't think we were gonna kill anybody!"

I growl. "Just tell me who you're working for."

Komo takes a shaky breath. "Ok." He begins. "It's-"

He's cut off by the sound of a ray gun being fired. A look of pain and shock quickly passes through Komo's eyes, and then he falls to the floor, dead. Behind him, a figure wearing a hood obscuring its face is holding a smoking ray gun.

"I'm sorry, old friend." The hooded figure says to Komo, lying on the ground with a deep laser wound in his back. "I didn't want it to end this way, but I won't let anyone get in my way."

He turns toward me "And I mean anyone."

I vaguely see a familiar impish grin from under the hood. A wave of realization, anger, and terror washes over me all at once.

"Rick?"

The man takes off his hood, and I see the familiar face of Rick Davis.

"Hello, Steven." He tells me.

"Welcome to The Revelation."

Thoughts collided in my head. Emotions

swirled in my heart. Of all the people it could have been, why Rick? The shadow man's words echo in my head, *"A friend of the old will betray your trust."* This is what that meant. My oldest friend betrayed me.

Before I could move, Rick switches a dial on his gun and shoots me with it. I feel pain course through my body, but I don't die.

"Oh, don't worry." Rick says, "I set it to stun, that way you can't escape."

"Why are you doing this?" I ask him.

He smiles his impish grin. "You have to be more specific, Steven."

"Why are you a terrorist? Why did you send that satyr, why do you want to kill me?" I ask almost all in one breath.

Rick smiles. "I don't see myself as a terrorist," he replies, "I see myself as the man who will lead the Watchers to a new revelation." He shows me a mark on his wrist, a red snake twisted around itself, so it forms an 8. The circles of the 8 transition into eyes.

I frown. "By exploding people?"

Rick shakes his head. "Ah, Jim. I never wanted

him to die. But he knew too much. He tried to stop us himself, so we blew him up. It wasn't my choice. A bit over the top if you ask me, but we got away with it for the most part."

I stare at Rick in disbelief. "What about the satyr?" I ask.

"Oh, Prem," Rick says. "When we came here, we told him that if he helped us catch you, we'd free Ullr from the grip of the Wicked Sun king in the north. Of course, we don't have any real intentions of doing anything like that yet, but m sure Prem will turn out alright."

I can't believe what I'm hearing. He tricked a poor satyr just to catch me.

After a long pause, I ask "Why do you want to kill me?"

Rick's face looks almost sad. "Steven, I don't want to kill you. That is the last thing I want to do!"

Confused, I ask, "Then what do you want from me?"

Rick smiles, his impish grin no longer seems friendly to me, just deceitful. "I want you to join us! Join the Revelation! We will make ourselves known to the multiverse! We will become gods!" He finishes his statement by throwing his hands up in triumph.

He looks back at me. "As you said, I could become the god of appreciation, giving appreciation where appreciation is due. Unlike Mr. K, who seems to hog all of it for himself."

So, this is what Rick has been planning all along. He wasn't kidding last night out on the balcony; he genuinely wants to become a god. "Watchers are about recording, so that we may learn and grow from the beneficial, and unfortunate, events of the multiverses," I say. "What you suggest is not what the Watchers are about!"

"Well, it should be!" Rick exclaims. He frowns and looks down at the floor. "I guess you won't be joining us then?"

I shake my head.

"Fine," Rick says sadly and angrily. "I can't bear to kill you myself, so I'll just leave you here to starve."

He goes to pick up the body of Komo.

"What are you doing with him?" I ask him before he leaves.

"Someone needs to take the blame for the explosion." He tells me without looking back.

Then he leaves me alone in the darkness.

For a while, I just sit alone in the cave. All seems lost and hopeless. Why should I even keep trying? My best friend wants to rule the Watchers. He'll turn in the body of Komo, claim that he was killed by a Natural Portal Maker, and start an all-out war. Why even try now? I can't escape even if I wanted to, and my hands are tied up, so I can't even make a portal. It's all lost. All I can do is sit in here and starve.

But then, I remember the Watcher HQ. I remember Níta sleeping peacefully on my bed. I remember Mr. K's smile, the kind of smile that makes him look almost like Santa Clause. I remember Mia, all those training sessions we've had, our talks over lunch, our time spent together. I can't let all that be destroyed...

Slowly, the feeling in my fingers return. I manage to turn on the tech plate on my right arm. Holographic images appear, slightly lighting up the room. I notice a small puddle of water in front of me reflecting the hologram off my arm, so I can see it. I dial the floating iPhone in my room, hoping that Níta will answer. After a few seconds, Níta picks up.

"Hello?" I hear her ask in a voice like she just woke up.

"Níta it's me!" I yell.

"Why are you calling your own phone?" she asks. "Did you leave behind something again?"

"No, listen Níta, I need your help."

I hear her voice perk up, "I'm listening." She says.

"I need you to take the dagger I keep in my drawer, and then go find Mia quickly. If it's after 9:00 she'll probably be at the Public Portal. Tell her that I'm stuck in a cave somewhere in Ullr, universal number, K^86*47:93264."

I hear her scribbling on a piece of paper. "So, let me get this straight. You want me, to take your dagger that I'm not allowed to touch, leave your room with said dagger, and go find Mia to travel to a different universe?!"

"Yes, except for that last part," I respond.

"What do you mean?" Níta asks.

"After you find Mia," I continue "I want you

to go back to my room, lock the door and stay in there."

There's a long pause. "Fine." She responds.

I breathe a sigh of relief. "Ok go, now!"

Níta hangs up the phone. I then sit quietly in the cave, waiting for my friends to arrive.

With a dagger hooked to her pants, and her potted sapling under her arm, Níta runs through the hallway toward the elevator. Once in, she rapidly presses the "Floor one" button. Anxiously, she watches the number of floors displayed on the screen in the elevator lower as she descends.

Finally, the doors open. She runs toward the public portal area. When she gets there, she finds that everyone is heading toward a crowd in the library. She walks over and sees someone standing on a table speaking to everyone. It's difficult to make out the person at first, so she makes her way toward the front of the crowd. Once there she realizes the person talking is Rick. Next, to him, someone seems to be lying down on the table.

"Today I found the one who had caused the explosion and death of Jim Welsh!" Rick begins.

He picks up the dead body of Komo Yong and

shows it to the crowd. The crowd gasps collectively, and many of the members begin to chat with each other. While this is going on, Níta notices a hooded man with a strange symbol resembling an 8 tattooed on the back of his hand.

Someone in the crowd yells, "Who killed him?"

Rick responds, "He was killed by Steven Black."

Níta's eyes widen in shock. The crowd begins to murmur again.

The hooded man looks up and yells "He was murdered by a Natural Portal Maker! They want to start their war!"

A few people yell in agreement.

But another figure, with his hood pulled down, stands up and says "But Komo was the one who caused the explosion!" a few other people yell in agreement with the second figure.

In just a few minutes, the whole crowd has gotten riled up by the epidemic. A few people try to stop the fighting but to no avail.

Amidst the fighting, Níta backs out of the crowd, and she notices that one of the people trying to stop the fighting is Mia. She runs over to her.

"Mia!" she exclaims.

Mia backs away from the crowd and runs over to Níta.

"Níta what are you doing here?!" She asks her.

"Steven called me, he told me to find you," Níta responds.

"Steven!?" Mia realizes, "Is he ok? Where is he? Did he really kill Komo?"

Níta shakes her head, "I don't know if he did or if he's ok, but I know where he is." She hands Mia the note she wrote. "We have to go now!"

They run toward the public portal and into the control room. Mia pushes some buttons on the control deck and the portal springs to life.

Before they enter, Mia stops and looks at Níta. "Wait, is Steven ok with you coming along?"

Níta thinks for a moment. Steven told her that she should stay in his room and lock the door. After seeing what happened in the crowd, it seems like it would be the safest option. But what if Steven is injured? She could heal him and prove that she could go out of the room more often!

"Yeah, he's cool with it." She lies.

Mia looks suspicious. "Ok, but you better not get me in trouble." She replies jokingly.

They both walk into the portal and enter Ullr.

I sit in the cave. I'm still mostly paralyzed from the ray gun that Rick shot me with. All I can do is whistle since my mouth, eyes, head, and fingers are the only things I can really move at this point.

How long has it been since I called Níta? Minutes? Hours? I'd lost track. All I'm certain about is that Mia and Níta will come for me. When? I don't have a clue. But I know they will come. Eventually.

I continue to sit in the cold dank cave. Until I hear footsteps coming in from the cave. I smile, expecting to see Mia. Instead, I see a monster. A giant caterpillar-like creature walks into the cave. It opens its mouth and lets out a roar like that of a raptor mixed with a spider.

"You're not supposed to be in Ullr!" I say.

The creature begins to charge at me. I close my eyes, ready to accept my fate. But then, I hear the sound of a blade slicing through flesh, and the monster gives one last screech and falls to the floor. I open my eyes and look up to see a dagger in the back of the creature's head, with Mia standing behind it in a position like she just threw a knife.

"Mia!" I yell. She looks at me, climbs over the dead creature, and hugs me.

"I was so worried about you!" she says still squeezing me to the point that it's hard to breathe.

"Oh, there's no need to worry, I'm fine!" I say.

She looks at me, "If you were truly fine, you would have gotten out of here by now."

I frown, "Yeah, I may have become a tiny bit paralyzed."

She shakes her head and laughs.

"Yeah, I figured." I hear a voice behind her say.

I look around her and see Níta standing on the dead caterpillar, arms crossed.

"Why are you here?!" I yell at her.

Níta shrugs, "Mia said I could come along."

I glare at Mia. She sticks her hands up defensively, "I asked her if you said she could!"

I sigh, "Alright, could one of you just cut me out of here?"

Mia nods. She turns and takes the dagger out of the monster's head and begins cutting at the ropes.

While doing so she asks, "So, what happened. Rick said that you killed Komo. Is that true?"

I look at the floor angrily. "I didn't kill him," I say. "He did."

Mia looks at me surprised, "Wait, Rick killed him?"

I nod. "He shot him while he was trying to cut me out of here. Rick is behind everything. He blew up Jim Welsh, sent a Satyr after me, and is trying to start a Watcher war!"

Mia frowns, "Well he may have succeeded."

I continue to stare at the floor as Mia cuts my ropes.

"I can't believe Rick would do all this." She says, "I can't even imagine what you're feeling right now."

I let out a small sigh.

Mia looks down. "I'm sorry, forget I said anything." Once she cuts through the ropes, she helps me to my feet. "Can you stand?" she asks me.

"I think so," I respond.

She lets go of my hand, only for me to immediately fall flat on my face.

"Ow," I say.

"Here," Níta says and she walks up to me.

She puts her hands on my back, closes her eyes, and concentrates. After a while, a pink aura glows around her hands. In about two minutes, I feel the paralysis wearing off.

"That's all I can do," Níta says. "You'll be able to stand but you'll need support while walking."

I slowly get up. "Wow!" I say, "Good job there Níta! You've become much better at healing magic."

She smiles and blushes a bit, but she does her best to hide it.

"Alright, let's just get out of here, I'm freezing," Níta says.

"How do you think I feel!?" I scoff.

With Mia supporting me, we walk out of the cave. As the blinding light of the outside world hits my eyes, Mia asks "Ok, you think you can create a portal?"

I respond, "Yeah, I think so." I hold one of my hands to the right of my head, and the other to the left of my hips. I concentrate as hard as I can, and I feel time and space tear open like paper. On the other side, I see a rippling version of my room. We all jump into the portal.

Once out of the portal, we exit into my room. I sit down on my bed, while Níta grabs her book of healing off the shelf. She flips through it to find what she needs to do to heal me completely.

"Ok, got it!" she says.

She runs over to my desk and opens the drawer, pulling out of seemingly nowhere a container of what looks like honey.

"I don't remember ever buying that," I say after she takes it out.

"Of course, you wouldn't! I bought it." She responds.

"Wait for what?!" I say. "With whose crowns?"

"Let's not discuss financial details right now!" Níta says quickly.

She walks over to me.

"Ok, so, I'm gonna pour this on you." She says to me while unscrewing the lid of the container she's holding. "Its gonna hurt. A lot."

Before I could say anything, she dumps the bottle over my head so that the goopy liquid oozes over my body. As soon as it touches me, pain shoots through my body. I have a sensation as if I'm being horribly burned and freezing to death all at the same time. I scream in pain. I faintly hear what I think is Mia running over to try and help me. Suddenly, I hear Níta say something like "Don't touch him!"

After a few seconds, the goop oozes off me and crawls back into its bottle. The pain stops as soon as the slime comes off.

I yell at Níta "Why do you even have that!?"

"For healing!" she responds.

I glare at her, confused and angry.

"In what universe is that considered healing?" I ask her.

She rolls her eyes. "Stand up." She tells me.

I stand, expecting to fall on my face again. Surprisingly, as I stand up, I begin to feel more exhilarated, like a pump of adrenaline was just shot into me.

"Oh, now I see how this is healing," I say.

"Just never do that to me!" Mia tells Níta.

Níta smirks. Mia turns toward me.

"So, what do we do now?" she asks.

I stop to think. I don't know how long I was

in that cave. By now Rick must have started the Watcher War and might even be preparing to take over the entire HQ. What exactly can I do? I quickly go over thousands of plans in my head, but none of them seem to work. But then I look at the desk crowded with enchanted items. Two items on the desk stand out to me, the bottle of the eternal flame I had collected from earlier, and a tube of Extracted Possibility that I did not remember putting there.

Written on the tube it says "I had a hunch you may need this. -K" along with a note with instructions for making a Possibility bomb. I Pull the enchanted kettle out of my bag.

I smile. I know exactly what to do. I turn to Mia and Níta. "I have a plan."

Rick walks through the library. Chaos rages behind him. He had done it. He had started the Watcher War. He had planned out this day for years. Finally, he will rule the Watchers the proper way. We won't just remain hidden and record from the shadows anymore, he thought. Instead, we will be prominent in the multiverse. We will be the all-seeing gods of the worlds of a billion! He had just wished that Steven was here.

He should have joined me. I didn't want him to die. I couldn't kill him myself, so I let that caterpillar thing eat him. We took it with us everywhere, and we no longer had any use for it. But Steven wouldn't see it like that.

Why did Steven have to see the world so differently? Couldn't he have just gone along with my idea? What, he couldn't have just been a supportive friend? He *was* my friend! I genuinely cared for him! Heck, I would have died for him! But no! He just had to be the Watcher assigned for bringing down The Revelation! Why couldn't it have been Mika? Or Caedmon? Or Komo? Or Billy? Why not Billy?! No one likes Billy! No one would have cared if Billy got eaten!

Well, there's no use crying over spilled milk. I just need to take down the 8 Watcher governors. Once I do that, I'll officially rule the Watchers. I guess I'll start with Mr. K.

Rick walked into Mr. K's office. The doors open, and he sees someone sitting down in Mr. K's swirly chair, facing backward.

"Mr. K," Rick said, "I know you might be busy, but I would like to speak with you."

As he says this, he takes his laser gun out from behind his back and sets the dial to "kill". The swirly chair spins around, and sitting in the chair, is Steven Black.

"Not right now, Rick," I say doing my best Mr. K impression. "I'm too busy contemplating how to take you down!"

I sit in Mr. K's chair, staring at Rick with a surprised look on his face. I'm so close to cracking up it's hard to keep it in. But that moment doesn't last for long as Rick raises his gun and shoots at me. I duck just in time for the laser to miss and burn a hole right through Mr. K's chair.

Rick continues to fire barely missing me and in turn, destroying stuff from around the room. Finally, I duck under the desk, lunge at Rick, and knock him off his feet. The gun falls out of his hands and I pick it up, pinning him to the floor.

"Whatever happened to you not killing me personally?!" I ask him.

"Well what did you expect me to do?" he responds.

"Um, not shoot me?"

Rick continues to struggle.

"What are you waiting for? Kill me!" he yells at me.

I lower the gun "I'm not going to shoot you, Rick." I tell him. "Just tell me, what exactly are your plans again?"

Rick looks at me, "Why do you want to know that?" he asks,

"I'm thinking about joining your little group." I tell him, as I rub my ear, "If I get a refresher, I might change my mind and take over the HQ with you!"

Rick looks at me strangely, "I don't know what game you're playing Steven, but..."

"Hey, just a quick summary alright?" I say, trying to sound sincere.

Rick sighs, "Alright."

I smile.

He takes me through the whole history of his little group, basically repeating what he told me in the cave.

When he finishes, I say, "So essentially, you are

a terrorist group who murders a bunch of people, got it."

Rick looks at me weird, "Wait I thought-"

"You hear that, guys!" I cut him off, "Rick here is a terrorist."

"We're not terrorists!" Rick yells.

After he does, he hears what sounds like his voice on a speaker echoing from outside.

Suddenly, a screen in Mr. K's room turns on and displays a live video feed of Mia and Níta.

"Oh, I heard loud and clear, Steven!" Mia says from the tv. "So, did the rest of the HQ!"

From outside the room, I hear the crowd murmuring.

"Rick's the one who did all of this!" someone says from the crowd outside.

"Billy's right!" another member of the crowd screams. "Let's get him!"

"How?!" Rick screams at me.

I tap my device in my ear. "Just a little technology!" I say.

Rick yells and somehow manages to throw me off him. I try to go and grab the gun, but he reaches it before me.

"Followers!" He yells, "Head to floor 31, room C:137! Kill Mia and that tree... kid... girl, thing!"

Níta says from the screen, "Wait, you don't know my name?! Dude, we've known each other for like, 7 yea-"

She's cut off by Rick shooting the screen, destroying it. He tries to shoot at me, but I quickly stand up and run out the door.

Níta looks through the peephole on the door. She sees the elevator doors open and multiple guys walk out wearing robes with small red blotches on their hands.

"Uh, Mia," Níta says.

Mia sticks up a hand. "Can't talk, hacking."

"No one says 'hacking' Mia, we're not on a 1980's earth." Níta shoots back.

"Shut up." Mia murmurs.

Níta looks out the peephole again and sees the men getting ever closer.

"Mia they're coming!" Níta yells.

"You think I don't know that?" Mia yells back.

Suddenly someone knocks at the door.

"No one's home!" Níta yells through the door.

The knocks start to get harder.

"Mia!" Níta yells.

"I'm working on it!" she yells back.

The banging at the door gets ever louder. Then, Níta hears a loud Zap! And the banging stops. She looks through the peephole and sees that the door now has a force field around it.

"You're welcome!" Mia says.

But immediately after, a red circle begins to make the door much hotter.

"Oh, no," Mia says.

"What is it?" Níta asks.

"They've got a laser!" Mia responds. "The force field will slow it down, but it'll get through eventually."

Níta thinks to herself for a moment. Then it hits her. She reaches into Steven's desk drawer and pulls out the ooze she used on him earlier. She then pulls out another container of a red glowing liquid. Taking a syringe, she fills it with the red liquid and pumps it into the ooze. The ooze turns a bright red and begins to vibrate violently.

"Um, what's it doing?" Mia asks.

Níta looks at her, "Mia, I'm gonna need you to make a portal."

"What!?" Mia yells.

"I just put a bunch of extracted anger into this thing. Once I throw it through the force field, it'll crack open and attack everything in sight."

Mia stares at her, "Why do you have extracted anger? Where'd you even get that?!"

Níta responds, "It doesn't matter. The point is, I need you to create a portal, so we can get out of here."

Mia starts to look like she might have an anxiety attack. "Níta I can't make portals anymore you know that!"

Níta stares her right in the eyes, "Mia I know you can. You don't even have to go to another world! Just teleport us to the other side of the Watcher HQ!"

Mia glares at her, "But what if I can't do it?"

Níta looks at her with a confident smile, "You can do it, Mia. I know Steven would say the same."

Mia looks up, "Ok, I'll try."

She goes and stands toward the left side of the room. She positions her arms and concentrates with all her might. She pictures the far end of the library, that's where she wants to go. Níta puts a hand on the doorknob and begins to count down.

"Three," she says.

Mia continues to concentrate.

"Two."

Mia feels something in front of her rip.

"One!" Níta yells as she cracks open the door and throws the canister of red ooze.

She immediately closes and locks the door. As she looks through the peephole, she sees the red ooze fill up the entirety of the hallway. The muffled screams of the men in robes can be heard from inside it. Níta hears what sounds like a rip, and sees Mia standing in front of a portal.

"You did it!" Níta yells!

Mia stares at the portal with a gaping mouth. "I-I did it? I did it! I opened a portal!"

Níta laughs, "Ok, come on! Let's grab your computer and go!"

Mia grabs her laptop and Níta grabs her sapling, so it doesn't suffocate in the ooze. They both hop through the portal right before the ooze cracks through the door and fills the entire room.

I run and run. I don't have any time to make a portal, so I just need to run. I don't know if Rick is behind me, but I know that he's trying to kill me, which is enough motivation to get me to run.

I run toward the meeting room. It seems like it would be the safest place in the HQ right now. I hop inside, but when I open the doors, Rick is already inside.

"How did you-" I'm cut off by him firing at me with his ray gun.

"You don't know everything about me, old friend." He says while he continues to fire at me.

I manage to dodge all his lasers, but one manages to scrape by my shoulder. My shoulder begins to burn. Before Rick can fire again, I reach up onto the wall and flick off the light switch. Total darkness fills the room.

Rick switches his gun to a new mode and pulls the trigger. Instead of a laser-firing out, the new mode turns the gun into a flame thrower. Luckily, he hasn't seen me yet. Suddenly, I hear a voice in my ear.

"Steven are you there?" it asks.

It's Mia!

"Yeah, I'm here!" I whisper. "Are you guys ok?"

"Yeah, we're fine" Mia responds.

I see that Rick hasn't seen me yet, and he starts heading toward the door. I realize that I can't let Rick escape, if I let him go, then he'll continue to hurt people.

"Mia, I need you to do something for me," I say,

"What do you need?" she asks.

"I need you to activate *it* for me."

Mia goes silent.

"Steven, where are you?" she says.

"I'm in close range of Rick," I tell her.

"Steven, I can't do that, I need you to get out of there."

"Just enter in the code, ok?"

She goes silent again.

"Ok," she says at last.

I hear her typing on her computer.

"Just promise me that you'll get out of there, ok?" she asks.

I don't answer.

"Steven? Are you still there?" She asks.

"Goodbye, Mia," I say and turn off the call before she can say anything else.

I draw my sword and power up its enchantment. The Norse symbols on the sword light up, and I run toward Rick. All in one motion, I knock the gun out of his hand, turn behind him, and place the sword up to his throat. Rick just stands there for a moment.

"Killed by the very sword that I gave to you." he chuckles. "Well, go on then, Steven."

I stand there for a second, and then I drop the sword.

"As I said before, I'm not going to kill you."

But then I pull out a tube of green slime. Ricks' eyes open wide.

"But this will." I say, "Command, bomb Enter." The slime begins to glow, and I drop it.

As soon as it hits the floor, a giant green fiery explosion careens through the room, blasting us toward the walls.

Somehow, I manage to survive. My vision is blurry, and a loud ringing courses through my ears.

While lying on the floor, I see Rick. He managed to survive as well, but he doesn't look as good. He seems to be missing an arm from the explosion. But then he pulls out a book. He opens the book and begins to read from it. Even though my ears are still ringing, I hear him speak in a strange unrecognizable dialect.

As soon as he is done reading, a portal opens next to him. But this portal is different. It glows red on the outside of it. Somehow, Rick stands up and he manages to step through the portal. While going through, it looks as if the portal is causing him pain. Once he reaches the other side, the portal closes.

I see the two meeting doors open. A giant man comes in, wading through the fire. He picks me up and carries me out. Then, the world darkens.

When I come to, I'm lying down in bed. I feel some bandages on my legs and face, but that's about it. I hear a beeping noise coming from a machine next to me. I look over to my right and see Mia and Níta sitting in a chair in front of the wall. They both look a little sad and worried, but they're talking to each other to try and keep their spirits up.

"Why the long faces?" I ask them sarcastically.

They both turn to me and their faces light up!

They run toward my side and hug me while Níta repeatedly yells,

"I knew it! I knew he wasn't dead!"

From outside the room, Mr. K peeks his head in. He smiles.

"Steven!" He says.

He walks in and pats me on the shoulder. "It's about time you woke up!"

I blink. "How long was I out?"

"Nine days!" Mia groans.

"Oh, wow," I say. "Now I see why you guys were worried."

"It's a miracle that you're still alive!" Mia says.

Mr. K says "I'm glad that you're alright, son. Mainly because we couldn't get this one here to leave the healing room!" He points to Mia with a little laugh.

I look at her. "You stayed in this room for nine days?!"

She blushes, "Hey someone had to make sure you stayed out of trouble!" she says.

"I was asleep. What could I have done?"

Mia shrugs, and smiles.

"Oh, and this little one here is the reason you're

in such excellent condition." Mr. K pats Níta on the back.

I stare at her. "You healed me?!"

"Of course!" She responds, "Why do you think you only have three Band-Aids on after suffering an explosion!?" We all laugh again.

After a few hours, I was in the clear to get out of the bed. I was even able to take one of the Band-Aids off.

Mia, Níta, and Mr. K sit outside the healing room waiting for me.

"You did it, Steven!" Mia says to me.

"Did what?"

"You single-handedly stopped the War of the Watchers!" she exclaims.

I blush. "Well, not single-handedly," I say.

"And Rick won't be able to bother us ever again!" Níta says.

I frown.

"What's wrong?" Mia asks.

"Ricks still alive," I answer.

"What?! How?" Mia exclaims.

"I don't know how I just know he is. I saw him escape through a portal after the explosion."

Mr. K turns serious, "While the miracles of El Qubekī may have saved Steven from the explosion, I fear that some other supernatural force may have kept Rick alive."

We all sit in silence for a moment.

"Either way," Mr. K changes the subject, "You did an excellent job stopping a terrorist group, in fact, I have something for you." Mr. K reaches into his coat pocket and pulls out a bright yellow orb.

Inside the orb, there's some sort of spinning 3d image that takes on a new form whenever you look at it from a different side.

I take the orb in my hand.

"The Orb of Possibilities." Mr. K says.

I look back at him with joy in my eyes.

"Go on." Mr. K says.

All my friends watch on in wonder as I silently make my wish to the orb. I wish for all my memories to return, I think.

The orbs glow dies, and the 3d image in the orb stays on a picture of a brain for a minute before the picture disappears in a flash of light.

I gasp.

All my memories suddenly return. It's like I've

been knocking at the door of my memories, and that for the first time the door has opened for me. But then the person who answered the door slapped me in the face before letting me in.

The glass ball falls to the floor with a loud "thunk." I fall back off my seat. Mia helps me up

"What happened?" She asks.

I stare at all of them for a moment.

"I'm a descendant," I say.

"What?"

I continue, "I'm a descendant of Dr. Spencer Black, founder of the Watchers."

Epilogue.

Rick falls through the portal into a cave. He groans in pain as he hits the floor. He notices that he has lost his arm in the explosion. Painfully, he takes out a book and flips through the pages with his remaining arm. Once he finds the right page, he recites the words written down.

The ink on the page crawls off and forms into a massive glob of slime. It begins to cover Rick.

He begins to yell in extreme pain as the slime absorbs him. After the slime oozes off, he is fully healed. His arm has even grown back.

He stands up and brushes himself off. As he is about to leave the cave, he hears breathing behind him. He turns around to see the shadow man halfway submerged in the ground.

"*Why are you here?*" he asks the shadow.

Because you have lost. Like I said you would.

Rick glares at the shadow man "*I have not lost yet!*"

You do not understand who I am yet. The shadow creature states, *You do not understand the true power of that book either.*

Rick glares at it angrily, "*I know full well who you are Grulikatu!*" Rick yells at the creature, "*and I know full well the power possessed by the Necothrahm!*"

Grulikatu growls. *Do not say the name of the book aloud! Otherwise, he might hear you.*

Rick shakes his head.

Grulikatu continues, *We are more similar than you think. As of now, I stand in a time yet to come for the multiverse's, "The End of all Worlds." All universes, all dimensions all timelines, and all worlds will cease to exist as if they had never occurred. We are a main player in that event, Rick, but not in stopping it.*

Rick continues to glare at the creature. "*Would you just leave me alone already?*"

Grulikatu nods and begins to crawl back into the ground, *You will not hear from me again, for I fear the risk of changing this timeline too much in the wrong way.*

Grulikatu fully emerges himself in the ground and disappears.

Grasping on to the Necothrahm, otherwise known as "The Book of *Thrack*," Rick shakes his head and vanishes from the cave.

J.O.WELCH

To be continued...

ACKNOWLEDGMENTS

First and foremost, I would like to thank God for blessing me with the mind and persistence for writing and publishing a book. I would also like to thank my grandparents; Papa, Grandma Michele, Grandma Lorie, Grami, Abuelito, and GG for donating and supporting this publication (Hope you all enjoy the signed copies!). My parents deserve a huge thanks as well, for always being there, giving me advice and suggestions, and supporting and encouraging me throughout this journey. A massive thanks to my brother, Josh, who stayed up late into the night on several occasions listening to my rambles about my stories and world-building. And a thank you to my little sister Serenity, who was an inspiration for one of the characters in my story. A continued thanks to Aronn, my

Nino, who designed the incredible cover and dealt with my pickiness and confusing descriptions during the early stages of sketching. To Mrs. Coman, a huge thanks as well, for inspiring me to write this "short" story. Additionally, a major thank you to Mr. Bunn who edited my story. Finally, I would like to thank all of my family, friends, and to each one reading this, who not only read through all of my story, but who also made it this far into the acknowledgments, for some reason. Thank you to absolutely everyone who helped me, supported me, and was just there with me during this incredible experience.

J. O. Welch was born in California to two loving parents. His hobbies include writing, reading, playing video games, eating, sleeping, and texting. He aspires to one day become a famous writer and is thrilled that he has managed to take the first step to (maybe) becoming one. Hopefully one day, he'll actually wake up on time so he can have more time to write.